S0-AOC-054

A Note to Parents and Caregivers:

Read-it! Readers are for children who are just starting on the amazing road to reading. These beautiful books support both the acquisition of reading skills and the love of books. In some books, there are common sounds at the beginning, the ending, or even in the middle of many familiar words. It is good preparation for reading to help students listen for and repeat these sounds as part of having fun with words.

The RED LEVEL presents familiar topics using common words and repeating sentence patterns.

The BLUE LEVEL presents new ideas using a larger vocabulary and varied sentence structure.

The YELLOW LEVEL presents more challenging ideas, a broad vocabulary, and wide variety in sentence structure.

The GREEN LEVEL presents more complex ideas, an extended vocabulary range, and expanded language structures.

When sharing a book with your child, read in short stretches, pausing often to talk about the pictures. Have your child turn the pages and point to the pictures and familiar words. And be sure to reread favorite stories or parts of stories.

There is no right or wrong way to share books with children. Find time to read with your child, and pass on the legacy of literacy.

Adria F. Klein, Ph.D.
Professor Emeritus
California State University
San Bernardino, California

Managing Editors: Bob Temple, Catherine Neitge
Creative Director: Terri Foley
Editors: Jerry Ruff, Patricia Stockland
Editorial Adviser: Mary Lindeen
Designer: Amy Bailey Muehlenhardt
Storyboard development: Charlene DeLage
Page production: Picture Window Books
The illustrations in this book were prepared digitally.

Picture Window Books
5115 Excelsior Boulevard
Suite 232
Minneapolis, MN 55416
877-845-8392
www.picturewindowbooks.com

Printed in the United States of America.

Library of Congress Cataloging-in-Publication Data
Blackaby, Susan.
The Word of the day / by Susan Blackaby ; illustrated by Amy Bailey
Muehlenhardt.
p. cm. — (Read-it! readers)
Includes bibliographical references.
Summary: When called upon by Mrs. Shay to pick the word of the day,
most students are distracted by their rumbling tummies, but Kat uses her
head instead.
ISBN 1-4048-0588-5 (reinforced library binding)
[1. Schools—Fiction. 2. Hunger—Fiction. 3. Food—Fiction. 4. Vocabulary—
Fiction.] I. Muehlenhardt, Amy Bailey, 1974- ill. II. Title. III. Series.
PZ7.B5318Wo 2004
[E]—dc22   2004004518

The Word
of the Day

By Susan Blackaby

Illustrated by Amy Bailey Muehlenhardt

Special thanks to our advisers for their expertise:

Adria F. Klein, Ph.D.
Professor Emeritus, California State University
San Bernardino, California

Susan Kesselring, M.A.
Literacy Educator
Rosemount-Apple Valley-Eagan (Minnesota) School District

PICTURE WINDOW BOOKS
Minneapolis, Minnesota

On Monday at 10:00, Mrs. Shay asked for the word of the day. She called on Jess.

Word of the Day

Monday:

Jess felt his tummy rumble.

Jess wanted a snack.

"The word of the day is *cheddar cheese*," said Jess.

"*Cheddar cheese* is two words," said Mrs. Shay.

"OK," said Jess. "The word of the day is just plain *cheese.*"

Word of the Day

Monday:

"Lots and lots of cheese," said Bob.

"Yum," said Sunny.

Mrs. Shay wrote *cheese* on the pad.

On Tuesday at 10:00, Mrs. Shay asked for the word of the day. She called on Vic.

Vic felt his tummy rumble.

Vic wanted a snack.

"The word of the day is *carrot sticks*," said Vic.

"*Carrot sticks* is two words," said Mrs. Shay.

Word of the Day
Monday:
      cheese
Tuesday:

12

"Carrot sticks and dip," said Jess.

13

"The word of the day is *dip*,"
said Vic.

"Lots and lots of dip," said Bob.

"Yum," said Sunny.

Mrs. Shay wrote *dip* on the pad.

On Wednesday at 10:00,
Mrs. Shay asked for the word
of the day. She called on Bob.

Word of the Day

Monday:
    cheese
Tuesday:
    dip
Wednesday:

Bob felt his tummy rumble.

Bob wanted a snack.

"The word of the day is *popcorn*," said Bob. "Lots and lots of popcorn." "Yum," said Sunny.

Mrs. Shay wrote *popcorn* on the pad.

Word of the Day

Monday:
  cheese
Tuesday:
  dip
Wednesday:
  popcorn

On Thursday at 10:00, Mrs. Shay asked for the word of the day. She called on Sunny.

Sunny felt her tummy rumble.

Sunny wanted a snack.

"The word of the day is *plum*," said Sunny.

"Big plums," said Vic.

"Yellow plums," said Jess.

"Black plums," said Kat.

"Lots and lots of plums," said Bob.

"Yum," said Sunny.

Mrs. Shay wrote *plum* on the pad.

On Friday at 10:00, Mrs. Shay asked for the word of the day. She called on Kat.

Word of the Day
Monday:
    cheese
Tuesday:
    dip
Wednesday:
    popcorn
Thursday:
    plum
Friday:

Kat had a sack. Kat pulled out a stack of crackers. Kat pulled out slices of cheese.

Kat pulled out carrot sticks and dip.

Kat pulled out a bag of popcorn.

Kat pulled out five big plums.

"The word of the day is *snack*," said Kat.

OOOOOOOOOOOOOOOOOOOOOOOOOOOOO

<u>Word of the Day</u>

Monday:
   cheese
Tuesday:
   dip
Wednesday:
   popcorn
Thursday:
   plum
Friday:

Mrs. Shay wrote *snack* on the pad.

Word of the Day

Monday:
   cheese
Tuesday:
   dip
Wednesday:
   popcorn
Thursday:
   plum
Friday:
   snack

"Yum," said Sunny.

Levels for *Read-it!* Readers

Read-it! Readers help children practice early reading
skills with brightly illustrated stories.

Red Level: Familiar topics with frequently used words and
repeating patterns.

I Am in Charge of Me by Dana Meachen Rau
Let's Share by Dana Meachen Rau

Blue Level: New ideas with a larger vocabulary and a variety
of language structures.

At the Beach by Patricia M. Stockland
The Playground Snake by Brian Moses
The Word of the Day by Susan Blackaby

Yellow Level: Challenging ideas with an expanded vocabulary
and a wide variety of sentences.

A Fire Drill with Mr. Dill by Susan Blackaby
Hatching Chicks by Susan Blackaby
Marvin, The Blue Pig by Karen Wallace
Moo! by Penny Dolan
Pippin's Big Jump by Hilary Robinson
A Pup Shows Up by Susan Blackaby
The Queen's Dragon by Anne Cassidy
Tired of Waiting by Dana Meachen Rau

Green Level: More complex ideas with an extended vocabulary
range and expanded language structures.

Classroom Cookout by Susan Blackaby
Clever Cat by Karen Wallace
Flora McQuack by Penny Dolan
Izzie's Idea by Jillian Powell
Naughty Nancy by Anne Cassidy
The Roly-Poly Rice Ball by Penny Dolan
Sausages! by Anne Adeney
Sunny Bumps the Drum by Susan Blackaby
The Truth About Hansel and Gretel by Karina Law

A complete list of *Read-it!* Readers is available on our Web site:
www.picturewindowbooks.com